The Dream Violin

The Dream Violin

AND OTHER STORIES OF FAMILIES
AROUND THE WORLD
Compiled by the Editors
of
Highlights for Children

CONTENTS

The Dream Violin

By Linda Crotta Brennan

It was 1909, and a cottage door opened in the little village of Pesaro, Italy.

"Thank you, Signor," said a music student from the academy. "You did a beautiful job of repairing my violin."

"A pleasure," replied Signor Druda. He returned to his shop and looked at the tools there—the tools of his trade as a carver. He thought of the doors he had carved for St. Anthony's Church and the few lira he had been paid for his hard work.

Suddenly, Signor Druda stomped into the kitchen and slammed his fist down on the table.

His daughter, Maria, sat looking through a box of postcards from her older sister, Enez, in America. She jumped when her father's fist hit the table.

"What is it, Papa?" she cried.

"I have just made a decision," Signor Druda announced. "I will not carve any more doors. I am going to make violins instead."

"But why, Papa?" asked Maria.

"It is something I have always dreamed of. And what is life if we never follow our dreams?"

His wife, Signora Druda, looked thoughtful. "Do you know how to make violins?" she asked.

"No, but I can learn. I am a carver, after all, and I have repaired many violins for the students at the academy."

"I will take in washing while you are learning," Signora Druda said firmly. "It will be just enough to put food on the table."

"I'll help," offered Maria.

"Certainly," agreed her mother. "You can carry water from the village fountain and gather wood for the fire. I'll need wood to boil the water for the washing."

So Signor Druda set to work, learning to carve violins. Soon he knew which wood to use for all the parts, and how to shave them to just the right shape and thickness. But no matter how hard he tried, he couldn't get the varnish exactly right, so his violins had a dull, flat sound.

While her papa sat mixing varnish in his workshop, Maria and her mother gathered dry wood, carried water, and boiled wash in a big black pot.

"I'm so tired, Mama," Maria complained one night. "Why can't Papa carve doors again?"

"Hush, please, Maria. Papa is making art, like Michelangelo and DaVinci. Such a dream is worth our hard work."

"I guess you're right, Mama," sighed Maria.

Signora Druda gave Maria a hug. "I just got a letter from Enez. Her husband got a job as a waiter in a fancy restaurant. She will be able to send money toward your passage with her next letter."

Maria sighed. She dreamed of joining her sister in America. She often tried to imagine the big, bustling city of New York, where Enez lived. But Enez could only send a little money at a time toward Maria's trip. It might be years before they had enough for her passage.

Just then Signor Druda burst into the room. "I've done it!" he cried, waving a violin in his hand. "Listen to the music!"

The violin had a skin as smooth as silk and sang with a voice like the angels.

"How did you do it, Papa?" asked Maria.

"It's the varnish," he said. "I've finally perfected the blend. It's a magic varnish!"

News of the violins with the angelic voices soon spread throughout the academy. Signor Druda worked long hours, filling the students' orders.

"Papa, you are working too hard!" complained Maria one day.

Signor Druda coughed and rubbed his chest.

"I'm fine, Little One. What's that delicious smell coming from your mother's pot?"

"Chicken cacciatora, Papa. This is the third time we've had meat this week!" said Maria as they sat at the table.

"It's doing you good. You're looking very well, Maria." Signor Druda started to smile, but he was shaken by another cough.

"The better Maria looks, the worse you look," said Signora Druda. "I don't like that cough. We should call the doctor."

"Nonsense," scoffed Signor Druda.

But the next day he was too sick to get up, even to work on his precious violins. So the doctor was called after all.

"What did he say?" Maria asked after the doctor had left.

Signora Druda wrapped Maria in her arms and held her close. "It's the varnish," she whispered. "The magic varnish. It has been poisoning him."

"What about Papa's violins?" asked Maria.

"There must be no more violins," Mama said.

"What will we do?" cried Maria.

"We will sell the violins Papa has already made and buy a ticket to America."

"America?"

"Of course." Signora Druda hugged Maria. "It's time for another Druda to follow her dream."

The violins sold quickly, and when the time came for Maria to leave, Signor and Signora Druda walked with her to the dock. She clung to her mother's hand.

"Mama. Papa. I am so scared!"

"Be brave, Maria," Mama said. "Enez will be there to meet you."

"But what about you?" Maria frowned. "What will the two of you do now?"

"I am much stronger," Papa assured her. "I will go back to my carving. I have made my violins, and I am satisfied now." He handed Maria a carefully wrapped package. "For you," her father said. "Here is a Druda violin. It will help you remember to follow your dreams."

The whistle blew. Time for one last hug and kiss, then Maria walked up the ramp to the ship.

"Good-bye, Maria!" called Signor and Signora Druda as the ship pulled out to sea.

"Good-bye, dear Mama and Papa," Maria said, holding her violin and looking back at the docks. "Already I have a new dream," she said to herself. "I dream that one day I will send for you, and you will come to visit me in America."

Totem Pole
for
Grandfather

By Russell Trainer

Tosona was eleven years old. He stood straight as a young tree, and he was quick-stepping as a deer. But today, as he moved through the village, he seemed to stoop from sadness, and each step came slower than the one before. When he reached the hut of the wood-carver, he paused, remembering how the old man was called Tishmian the Terrible because of his bad temper. And Tosona remembered how it was often said that the old man would long ago have been run out of the village if it were not for his talent as a wood-carver. The greatest chiefs engaged Tishmian to do their totem poles. "And now," Tosona thought, "I must face him again." He straightened and walked into the hut.

Tishmian was chipping at a new log of red cedar. He looked up.

"You again, Tosona," the wood-carver said. "Go away. Don't bother me."

"Please, have you changed your mind?" the boy asked. "Will you carve for my grandfather?"

"I carve for chiefs, not the poor."

The boy moved closer and squatted beside Tishmian. "I'll tend to the traplines for you. I'll fish and hunt for you."

"No," the old man roared. "Go away."

Tosona started to say more, but instead stood up and left.

When he was near his hut, he stopped and sat down on a log. His expression was much too unhappy for an eleven-year-old boy.

Soon Tosona heard a sound and saw Nootka hurrying toward him. They had been friends since they were babies, and now they liked to race and swim together. But today he wasn't happy to see her. She was the grandchild of Tishmian, who had refused him a totem pole.

"Did you see my grandfather?" she asked.

"Yes. He refused again. He chased me out."

The girl stared sadly at the ground. "I'm sorry, Tosona. The chiefs have spoiled Grandfather."

The boy shook his head slowly. "I must give my grandfather a gift. He has raised me and denied himself everything. He has dreamed of a family totem. And if my parents had not died in the storm, Grandfather would have his dream. We would have riches, and Grandfather would have his totem."

Nootka nodded her head. "I know, Tosona."

The boy stood up. "I should leave."

"May I visit with you and your grandfather?"

"No. You are Tishmian's grandchild. Please don't come to us anymore," said Tosona sadly as he walked away.

When Tosona finished the day's chores, he made his grandfather comfortable on a pile of brightly colored blankets. "Grandfather, I'm going to the river. The fish are biting."

The old man nodded. "Go ahead. I'll be fine."

Tosona patted the blankets again, then he turned and left.

At the river, Tosona pushed the canoe from the shore and swung lightly aboard. He paddled toward a favorite fishing spot.

When he rounded the jutting section of the shore, he saw a small figure. It was Nootka, and she was swimming alone among the boulders. "Crazy granddaughter of a mean wood-carver," he thought to himself. "If she moves too far out, the current can carry her to the rapids." He continued paddling, ignoring the girl.

He looked back as his canoe nosed ahead. She seemed to be waving to him. Then he saw that it had happened. Nootka was being pulled toward the rapids.

In three quick strokes Tosona turned the canoe about and headed toward Nootka. He pulled the canoe even with her, carefullly stood up, and dived into the cold water.

His dive had been well planned. He found Nootka while still beneath the water. He grabbed her under the arms. Then, with great kicks and strokes, they swam against the strong current.

When they reached shore, they lay on the sand, breathing deeply. Finally Tosona stood up and said, "Go home, Nootka." He turned and walked toward the village.

The next morning Tosona had just stepped outside the hut when he saw Tishmian and Nootka approaching. The old man was walking fast and puffing as he called, "Tosona. Wait."

Tosona noticed that the old man's face seemed different. It was softer, and the eyes were not so cold-looking.

"I am sorry I refused you the totem pole," Tishmian said. "You saved Nootka. Thank you."

The boy did not answer.

"And—you shall be rewarded. Your grandfather will have a totem." Tishmian stepped closer to the boy and put his hands on his shoulders. "But you honor him more than a thousand poles could." The old man turned and walked away.

Tosona sat down by his hut. His eyes glowed with a happiness he had not known for a long time. Shyly Nootka sat down next to him.

Tosona looked at her. "There is something I don't understand," he said. "You're a strong swimmer, but I had to pull you from the river. And you helped swim to shore. Besides, you know about the danger of that current."

"Yes, but you rescued me," she said, smiling in an amused and secret way.

The boy scowled at her. "Crazy granddaughter of Tishmian. I wouldn't be surprised if you—"

"May I visit your grandfather now?" she interrupted quickly.

Tosona stood up and moved aside to let her pass. "Yes. Come in." He had a confused look as he watched Nootka enter the hut. Then he shook his head and followed her.

Isao's Fish

By Mary Branch

When Isao looked out the big window of his family's new apartment, he felt as though he were in a forest of tall buildings. Looking down from the fourth floor, he could see a playground in the center of this apartment-forest. There were swings and slides and a sandbox. There was even a small goldfish pond nearby where children could kneel and watch the fish.

But Isao did not like this new home. He wished his *o-tō-san* (father) and his *okā-san* (mother) had not decided to move from their quiet little house. Here people were always going up and down the wooden steps to their apartments. Their heavy shoes made a loud sound on the wooden steps— *klang-klong, klang-klong!* So many boys and girls ran up the steps that Isao was frightened. He clung to the side of the stairway so they could pass without touching him.

All day long children shouted and played. A tall boy tried to wave him over to join their game, but Isao did not know any of them. At first his mother went to the playground with him. Then she told him he could go and play by himself.

"I don't want to play with them, *Okā-san*. I have a book to read."

She looked at him. "You should go out and play in the sunshine."

"Later," he said. He read his book, then read it again. In the evening Isao's father put on his kimono and sat in his big chair to read the newspaper. Isao stretched out on the *tatami* and looked at the comic section, although he could not read all of the words.

"Isao-chan reads too much," his mother said.

"There are lots of children to play with here," his father said. "You should play outside before the cold weather comes."

Isao wished he were a cricket. He pretended he had not heard his father. He rattled the pages of the newspaper. When he looked up, his father stared at him for a moment.

"We will settle this later," his father said, and returned to his newspaper.

On Sunday his parents took Isao for an outing. They rode the bus all the way to the seaside. Isao played in the sand and waded in the surf. His father played with him. His mother had a basket of food. She had *sushi,* made of rice and vegetables wrapped in seaweed. They had little *mochi* cakes that his mother had made from steamed rice that had been pounded into paste. They were sweet and very good. Isao wished they could go on such an outing every day.

When they returned home, Isao's father took him to the playground. They knelt on the edge of the fish pond and watched the golden carp swim slowly about.

"I'll ask the manager if I may donate a fish to the pond," Isao's father said.

In a few days he came home with a package. Isao looked into the container and saw a beautiful golden fish. It was almost as big as the space it tried to swim in.

"Is it for me?"

"For you and all the people in the apartment building. We will go and put it into the pond."

Isao and his parents went down the stairs. His father's shoes klang-klonged. Isao made his do the same. His mother's straw *zori* made a soft, swishing sound. They took the fish to the pond.

Isao's father opened the little container and poured the fish into the water. At first it splashed its tail, then it remained very still. A fish that lived in the pool came close to stare at the new fish. Isao's fish darted to the far side of the pool. It found a water reed and hid from the other fish.

"It will soon make friends with the fish who live in the pool," *O-tō-san* said.

Isao and his father and mother sat by the pond and watched their fish for a long time. The fish hid behind the reeds, peeking out at its strange neighbors. After a long time it gently swam part way out. The other fish darted back and forth near the new fish. Each time, it zipped back into its hideout. But after a while Isao saw his fish ease its way close to another golden carp. Sunlight played on their sides as the two fish swam around the pond together.

"My fish looks so much like the others I can hardly tell which one it is," Isao said.

"That's right," his father said. "When fish swim together, they have no great difference."

As they walked back to their home, Isao stopped by the playground. A tall, bright-eyed boy smiled at him. It was the same one who had invited him to join their game.

"May I stay and play with that boy?" Isao asked.

His father and mother smiled and nodded. Isao walked toward the boy, his shoes going *klang-klong, klang-klong* on the hard walk. Then he laughed at the noise, and the boy laughed, too. Isao jumped into the sandbox with his new playmate.

A Viking Farewell

By Iva F. Kaiser

Ryan mourned the passing of his grandfather. He clenched and unclenched his hands. His eyes burned from the tears he had shed. Though Grandpa Gus had been a gruff man, Ryan knew he would have understood.

Ryan turned and walked back into the cabin. His grandparents had built this cabin when Ryan's dad was small. The family had spent vacations and weekends here, even after Grandma Erikson had died. Grandpa loved fishing in the lake. As soon as Ryan was old enough to hold a fishing rod, Grandpa Erickson had put one in his hand.

Mother and Aunt Grace were putting lunch on the table. Ryan's mother glanced at him as the screen door slammed shut.

"We'll be eating soon. Have you seen Dad and Uncle Ted?"

Ryan shook his head. "Not for a while."

Seeing the pained expression on Ryan's face, his mother said, "Ryan, I'm sorry. But you know we can't have your grandfather's funeral the way he wanted it."

Ryan flung himself on the sofa. He picked up a pillow that his grandfather had used when he took an afternoon nap. "But Mom, Grandpa said he wanted a Viking funeral."

Grandpa Gus had been proud of his Norwegian ancestry. He loved to tell Ryan about the exploits of Erik the Red and Leif Eriksson.

Aunt Grace sat beside Ryan. She patted his hand. "He was my father, Ryan. I know that his Norwegian forefathers and their history were important to him."

"Then why can't he have what he wanted?" Ryan asked angrily.

"You're only making things harder," his mother said as Uncle Ted and Ryan's dad came in. "This is a sad time, and we don't want to spend it arguing with you." She sighed. "Let's have some lunch."

Ryan ate very little. He excused himself and went to the bedroom that used to belong to Grandpa Gus. Shelves on the wall displayed an array of model Viking ships that his grandfather had lovingly carved.

Once Grandpa had told Ryan about the ship that Norsemen called the *skuta.* It was used on exploratory voyages, and it was wide and deep enough to hold supplies for long journeys. But Ryan's favorite was a warship with a beautiful painted dragon's head for the prow. Grandpa said it was called a *knorr.*

Ryan held the ship in his hands, remembering a day not so long ago when he and Grandpa sat on the bank of the lake. Grandpa had seemed tired lately and was content to sit on the shore rather than doing chores.

In his deep voice, Grandpa Gus had broken the silence. "Ryan, sometimes I imagine this lake is a *fjord* in Norway. When my imagination gets going, I see myself standing in the prow of a Viking ship. There's a fine leather helmet on my head and a sturdy wooden shield in my hand. The oars manned by my crew are cutting through the water. We are going to discover new lands."

"Grandpa, I imagine I'm going with you," Ryan said eagerly.

Grandpa put his arm around Ryan. "I'd like that very much." Then his smiling face had become more serious. "One day, Ryan, we all must take a journey," he said.

"What do you mean, Grandpa?"

Grandpa puffed on his pipe.

"When we die, we take a journey." He smiled. "Don't look sad. Death isn't feared when you are older like me. Besides, I will be with your grandmother again." Grandpa got up slowly. He gazed across the lake. "I have told your Dad and the rest of the family that I'd like a Viking funeral."

Ryan tried to overcome the shock of hearing Grandpa talk about dying. "A Viking funeral?"

His grandfather told him that when a Viking chieftain died, his body was put in a boat, set afire, and cast out to sea.

Ryan's thoughts were interrupted when his dad came into the bedroom. "It's almost time for the funeral," he said. "Son, you have to understand that there are laws regulating burials. The Viking type of funeral is not allowed these days."

After the funeral and procession to the cemetery, family and friends came back to the cabin to have something to eat, and to remember the good times they had shared with Gus Erikson.

Ryan went to Grandpa's room and stood gazing at the ships. He reached for the ship with the dragon's head. On his way out of the room, he saw his grandfather's pipe and took the pipe, too. He picked up a box of matches lying on the desk.

No one noticed as Ryan left the cabin. When he reached the shore of the lake, Ryan placed the pipe inside the model ship. The ship's small sail billowed in the breeze.

Ryan whispered, "This is the best I can do, Grandpa."

He reached into his pocket for the matches. As a match flared into flame, Ryan touched it to the sail. Giving the little ship a push with a long stick, Ryan let the breeze do the rest. The flames were burning faster, and the dragon's head seemed to be spitting fire.

"Have a safe journey, Grandpa Gus," Ryan said. Again the tears came.

Ryan heard a noise and turned around. His parents were there. His mom and dad walked up to him, and each put an arm around his shoulders.

"Ryan," his father said softly, "Grandpa Gus would say this is a fine Viking farewell."

Sasha and Her Family

By Mary Skwiot

Once there was a little girl named Sasha who lived with her family in a small village in Russia. Sasha and her family were very happy.

Each morning, Sasha would wake up happily, her dark eyes bright, and wait for the day to begin. She would lie in bed, picturing her mother at the stove, and she could smell the freshly baked rye bread. That made her hungry.

Sasha was sure their stove was the biggest in all Russia. It stood in the middle of the kitchen and covered half of the room. Sasha's father had promised that someday she could sleep on the flat shelf that stretched over the top. Sasha knew that many families used these shelves as bunk beds. Russian winters are very cold. Sasha liked to imagine sleeping on the shelf, wrapped in a quilt.

Some mornings when Sasha came downstairs, her father would hold out his arms and whisper, "Be careful, *Mala Mash* (which meant little mouse). Someone may put you in a cage." The cage was her father's arms.

Sasha would shake her head and laugh. "But that someone has to catch me." It was a game they played. Sasha liked it very much.

And then one day something happened that worried Sasha very much. It worried Sasha so much that her dark eyes grew troubled and sad. All that day . . .

Sasha would not laugh;
she would not smile;
she would not talk;
she would not even play with her dog, Kola,
which was too bad because that made Kola sad.
It all started that morning when Sasha,
her big sister, Nadja,
her little sister, Luba,
her big brother, Misha,
and her little brother, Kosha
sat down to breakfast.

Sasha's mother said:
  "Nadja, please drink your milk."
  "Luba, please stop playing with your spoon."
  "Misha, please eat your eggs."
  "Kosha, please sit up straight."
But she said nothing to Sasha. When Sasha's
father left for work,
  he kissed Nadja first,
  then Luba,
  and Misha,
  and Kosha,
  and Sasha last.
At school that day, Sasha was so worried
  she would not read her book;
  she would not write her words;
  she would not sing her songs;
  she would not play with her best friend, Majna.
After school, Sasha's mother scolded:
  "Nadja, please put your books away."
  "Luba, please pick up your toys."
  "Misha, please stop fighting with Kosha."
  "Kosha, please stop fighting with Misha."
But she said nothing to Sasha.
When Sasha's father came home,
  Nadja took his coat.
  Luba took his hat.
  Misha took his gloves.
  Kosha took his scarf.
  And Sasha hid behind a chair.

That night, when they sat down to eat, Sasha's family talked. They talked about what they did that day.

"I wrote a poem," said Nadja.

"I painted pictures with my fingers," said Luba.

"I sang the loudest in my class," said Misha.

"I played ball," said Kosha.

Sasha's mother and father looked at Sasha, but Sasha said nothing.

After dinner, Sasha's father asked, "Who would like a story?"

"I would like a story about a hen," said Nadja.

"I would like a story about a goose," said Luba.

"I would like a story about a bear," said Misha.

"I would like a story about a fox," said Kosha.

Sasha's father waited, but Sasha said nothing. Then he said:

"Tonight I will tell you a story about a family."

Sasha's father held up his hand. "What do you see?" he asked.

"Your hand, Father," said the children.

"That is right," said Father, "and what is it that makes up my hand?"

"Your fingers, Father," said the children.

"Right again," said Father. "Now, if I were to lose a single finger, do you not think I would miss that finger as much as any other? And if one finger should hurt, would I not feel the same pain, no matter which finger it was?"

The children listened as their father continued.

"Well, my children, it is that way with a family. *Each* of you five children is like a finger on a hand. Each is just as important—no more, no less—and each is just as needed and loved."

That night, before the children were tucked into bed, Sasha came to her mother and father.

"What is it, my little one?" asked her father.

"I did not think you loved me as much as the others," said Sasha.

"And why is that?" asked her father.

"Mother didn't talk to me at breakfast," said Sasha.

"But that is because you ate all your food," said her mother with a smile.

"And this morning, you kissed me last, Father," said Sasha.

"But that is because you did not push as hard as your brothers and sisters," said her father.

"And, Mother, you did not scold me as you did the others," said Sasha.

"But that is because you did everything just right today," answered her mother.

Sasha stopped worrying.

She began to laugh.

She began to smile.

She began to talk.

Sasha talked so much her mother had to scold her: "Sasha, please stop talking so much."

Sasha was happy again, and that was good.

Chopsticks

By Carol Hsu

Sun Lee put on his baseball hat and looked in the mirror. More than anything else, that baseball hat made him feel "all-American." It was blue and decorated with the emblem of his favorite team. Sunny stood up a little straighter whenever he thought about being an American. It seemed like years ago, instead of just seven short months, since he and his parents and Grandmother Lee had boarded the ship in Hong Kong Harbor and sailed for the United States.

Sunny raced down the stairs. "Good morning, Father," he said as he slid into his place at the breakfast table.

"Good morning, Sunny," Father answered.

"Good morning, Mother," said Sunny as his mother put a bowl of cereal at his place.

"Good morning, dear. Eat your cereal now or you'll be late for school."

"Good morning, Grandmother Lee," said Sunny politely. Grandmother Lee smiled across the table at Sunny.

"*Ho ma,* Sun Lee," she said cheerfully.

Sunny sighed softly as Grandmother went on eating her rice. Grandmother always spoke Chinese. And she ate rice for breakfast, lunch, and dinner just as she had done in Asia. Sunny finished his cereal and carried his dishes into the kitchen. "Mother," he asked, "why doesn't Grandmother learn to speak English? We're in America now! She might even like breakfast cereal in the morning if she'd only try it."

"Sunny," said Mother slowly, "Grandmother lived all her life in Hong Kong, and although she likes it here, sometimes she feels lonely. Perhaps you should speak Chinese when talking with your grandmother."

"But, Mother," said Sunny.

Mother didn't answer. She looked a little sad. "Better hurry or you'll be late for school," she said.

When the school dismissal bell rang that afternoon, Sunny dashed out to his locker, put on his baseball hat, and grabbed his glove.

"Here comes our number-one shortstop," Rich yelled as Sunny came onto the field. Sunny smiled with pride.

"Play ball!" yelled the coach. It was a good game, and the boys talked about it excitedly all the way home.

"Hey, Sunny," Rich said suddenly, "let's stop off at your house. We always go to Tom's house, and we've never even seen your room."

"Well," said Sunny, "It's sort of late . . ."

"OK," said Rich, "maybe another time."

The boys split up at the corner and Sunny walked on alone. When he pushed open the back door, Grandmother Lee was just taking a tray of Chinese bows out of the steamer. She fixed a plate for Sun Lee, smiling and humming all the while. The bows tasted so good—all soft white bread on the outside and steaming roast meat on the inside. Sunny licked his lips, but he was glad that Tom and Rich hadn't come home with him. American boys liked cookies after school. Tom's mother baked delicious cookies with little bits of chocolate in them. Maybe Grandmother Lee could learn to bake chocolate-chip cookies, and then he'd invite his friends over. But Grandmother wouldn't do that, Sunny thought gloomily.

The next day Sunny opened his eyes to see rain dripping down the windowpane. No baseball today, he thought as he went down the stairs.

"Good morning, Father," said Sunny. "Where's Mother this morning?"

"She's not feeling well today, Sunny, so she's staying in bed."

Just then Grandmother Lee came in with two steaming bowls of rice porridge.

"Looks good!" said Dad.

Sunny frowned. Rice for breakfast just isn't American, he thought. But then he noticed Grandmother's sad face, so he ate quickly and ran for his jacket.

Sunny grabbed his lunch box and dashed for the door. It felt heavier than usual. Sunny thought, "Grandmother probably put in twice as much as Mom does. She's always telling me to eat more."

At lunchtime the boys sat down by the window and glumly watched the rain pounding against the glass. "No game today," said Rich.

"We'd get soaked," said Tom.

"Hey, Sunny," said Rich, "I've got peanut butter again. Want to trade?

"OK," said Sunny as he opened his lunch pail to reach for the familiar plastic-bagged sandwich.

"Oh, no," groaned Sunny. He felt his face grow hot with embarrassment.

"Hey, what are those?" asked Rich in surprise.

Sunny tried to laugh. "They're chopsticks," he said. "My mother's sick, and Grandmother fixed my lunch. She doesn't know that kids don't eat with chopsticks in America."

"What's the bowl for?" asked Tom. "And what's this?" he asked, reaching for a small container.

Sunny knew the container was filled with bits of meat and vegetables. And he knew without looking what was in his thermos. "Rice," he groaned. "Rice for lunch."

"Well," said Tom, "what are you waiting for?"

"Can you really eat with those chopsticks?" asked Rich.

"Sure," said Sunny. He poured the rice into the bowl carefully, hoping no one else would notice. Then he picked up his chopsticks in one hand and his bowl in the other and began to eat.

"Say," said Rich when Sunny had finished, "that's really neat. Could I try the chopsticks?" Sunny handed them over to his friend. Rich tried to pick up a bit of bread crust, but each time it fell onto the table.

Tom laughed. "Let me try," he said. But Tom couldn't do it either.

Sunny began to laugh, too. "It's easy," he said, "Just hold one chopstick steady, as you would hold a pencil. Then hold the other chopstick with your thumb and index finger, so it pivots like this." Sunny demonstrated several times.

"I did it!" shouted Rich when he finally got the bread crust to his mouth.

Other children came to see what all the excitement was about. Everyone wanted to learn to eat with chopsticks. When the bell rang, Sunny had to promise to bring his chopsticks tomorrow, too.

After school, the boys rushed outside to find the sun shining brightly. "It's still too muddy to play ball," said Rich.

"Let's go to my house," said Sunny suddenly.

When the three boys burst into the kitchen, Grandmother Lee looked up in surprise. Then a smile spread across her face. "Good . . . morn . . . ing," she said cheerfully.

Sunny hugged his grandmother and laughed. "It's afternoon now, *Po-po*," he said. "But could we have some of your wonderful steamed bows?" The boys gathered around the table and Grandmother Lee gave them each a glass of milk and a steaming bowl.

"Wow!" said Rich. "This is delicious."

"Are you ever lucky," said Tom to Sunny.

"I am," said Sunny, smiling at his grandmother.

Not Yet, Kossiwa

By Marileta Robinson

Kossiwa sat on a stool watching her mother cook supper. Delicious smells were coming from the pot her mother was stirring. "Mother, let me help you make supper," said Kossiwa.

"No," said her mother, wiping her brow. "You are not yet big enough."

Kossiwa sighed. Her older sister sometimes got to fix a meal all by herself, and she didn't seem so much bigger than Kossiwa. When would Kossiwa be big enough?

"I know," she thought. "I will find something important to do. Then Mother will see that I am big enough to make supper."

Kossiwa went outside to look for something to do. Beside the door she saw her little sister, Kwakuvi, playing in the sand. Kwakuvi had made a little cookstove out of rocks and was stirring some leaves in a tin can.

"Kossiwa, can you come and play with me for a while?" called Kwakuvi.

"No, I can't. I'm going to do something important," said Kossiwa.

Kossiwa saw her grandfather working in the field next to the house. He was planting onions. That was important. "Grandfather, let me help," she said.

"No, Kossiwa, you are not big enough," said Grandfather. He held up a tiny onion. "These onions must be planted right, or they will not grow. You cannot help me yet."

Kossiwa heard the sound of a sewing machine coming from her Aunt Freda's house. She ran to see what her aunt was doing. Her aunt was a tailor and made clothes for other people. She was sewing a blouse.

"Auntie, please let me help you make the blouse," said Kossiwa.

"Oh, no, Kossiwa," said Aunt Freda, smoothing out a ruffle with her finger. "This blouse must be made just so, or the lady will not pay for it. You can help me when you are bigger."

As Kossiwa left Aunt Freda's house, she smelled something warm and sweet. She knew what that meant. Her grandmother was baking cookies to sell at the market. She ran to her grandmother's house. The courtyard was full of trays of cookies set out to cool.

"Grandmother, let me help you make cookies," said Kossiwa.

"No, Kossiwa," said Grandmother. "These cookies must be made just right, or they will not taste good. Then the people will not buy them. I'm sorry. When you are bigger, you can help me."

Grandmother gave Kossiwa a sack of cookies to take home to her mother.

When Kossiwa walked into her own courtyard, she saw a pile of dirty dishes. Her heart sank. It was her job to wash the dishes when her mother was finished cooking. Kossiwa had forgotten. What would her mother think?

Kossiwa took a bucket and got some water from the well. Then she got some clean sand and soap and settled down to wash the dishes.

"These dishes must be washed just right," she thought, remembering what Grandfather, Aunt Freda, and Grandmother had said. "If they are not clean, no one will want to use them."

She picked up the dirtiest pot and rubbed wet

sand around in it with her fingers until she had scrubbed off all the bits of food. Then she scoured it again with soap. Finally, she rinsed it with clear water. When she had finished, the pot gleamed almost as if it were new.

Kossiwa scrubbed the rest of the dishes and spoons until they shone, and then stacked them neatly and put them away.

The next day her mother called her to come into the courtyard. Kossiwa saw two cooking pots sitting on charcoal stoves. There was the big one her mother always cooked in, and there was a small one. Kossiwa's mother smiled.

"You did such a good job on the dishes yesterday, I think maybe you are big enough to learn to cook," she said. "I will cook in the big pot, and you may cook in the small one. Then, if you make a mistake, you are the only one who will have to eat it."

First, Kossiwa's mother showed her how to make a fire in the stove. Then she gave her some oil to pour into the pot. When the oil was hot, they each put tomato paste, fish, vegetables, water, and spices into their pots.

Kossiwa could hardly wait for her stew to finish cooking. At last her mother said it was done. Kossiwa broke off two pieces of bread and dipped them into her pot of stew. She took one and she handed one to her mother.

"No, it's your stew," said Mother. "You taste it first."

Kossiwa took a bite. She grinned. It was delicious! Then Kossiwa's mother tasted the stew and smiled. At that moment, Kossiwa must have been the proudest girl in all of Togo.

The Many-Colored Serape

By Gail Tepperman Barclay

Carlos Ramirez sat all alone on top of the mountain, his hands clasped about his knees. It wasn't right, he told himself miserably. How would the Johnson family know how very grateful he was if he didn't give them a gift?

Carlos's mother had thought the same thing six months before, when Carlos had left Mexico to come to the United States on an exchange program.

"You will be living with the Johnsons in their home," she had told Carlos. "It is customary for a guest to give a little gift of thanks to his host. Here, this is for the Johnsons." And she had handed him a serape.

The serape was the size of a blanket, woven neatly of brightly dyed wool. Carlos knew how long his mother had worked at the design. It was the finest serape he'd ever seen, and he was proud to be bringing the Johnsons such a beautiful gift.

But after Carlos had seen the Johnsons' house with its curtains, soft carpets, and big glass windows, the serape did not seem so special after all. Instead of giving it to the Johnsons, Carlos had folded it up and tucked it away in the far corner of his closet. It had remained hidden there for six long months.

Tomorrow morning, Carlos would be going home. Sitting very still, he took a long last look at the shimmering blue sea. California was very different from Mexico, he thought. Of course Mexico was his home, and he loved the great wide deserts and the brilliant sunrise and sunset. But California, with its green mountains and blue sea, was beautiful, too.

Carlos shivered. The sun was sinking rapidly, and it was beginning to grow chilly on the mountaintop. He got to his feet. He did not know what to do. He could not possibly give the Johnsons such a poor gift as the serape. And yet, what else could he give them?

He began to make his way down the mountain. Once on level ground, he ran the rest of the way to the house so he wouldn't be late for dinner.

Mrs. Johnson was frosting a big chocolate cake when Carlos came into the kitchen. "Hi, Carlos," she smiled. "Are you excited about going home?"

"I don't know whether to be happy or sad," he admitted. "Of course, I will be happy to go home and see my mother again. But I'm going to miss you and Mr. Johnson and Ken. Won't I look funny, crying and laughing at the same time?"

Mrs. Johnson patted him on the shoulder. "No crying," she told him, "just smiles. We're friends, and friends never really say good-bye—not in their hearts." She smiled at him, and Carlos smiled back. "Now you run upstairs and wash up for dinner. And tell Ken to hurry. Tonight's his night to set the table."

Carlos went quickly upstairs. Ken was in their room, working on a model airplane. He looked up as Carlos came in.

"I know." Ken grinned. "Mom wants me to set the table."

Carlos grinned, too, and nodded.

Ken stood up. "I guess I'd better get it over with," he said, leaving the room to go downstairs.

Carlos looked carefully around the room that he shared with Ken. It was a nice room, Carlos thought. And Ken Johnson was a wonderful friend. Carlos went to the closet and removed the serape from its hiding place. It WAS a beautiful serape, he thought. All the colors of Mexico were woven into it. There was the blue of the morning sky, the rich yellow of the desert sand, the dark green of barrel cactus, and the blazing red of the sunset. Yes, it was beautiful, but it just was not a fine enough present for the Johnsons.

The farewell dinner that Mrs. Johnson had prepared was so much fun that Carlos found himself laughing and joking with the family in spite of his troubled feelings. Finally, Mrs. Johnson carried in the chocolate cake. Carlos's eyes grew wide. Written across the top of the cake in pink icing were the words "To Carlos."

"Thank you," breathed Carlos. "Thank you. I wish—" but he could not go on.

"What?" asked Ken. "What do you wish, Carlos?"

"I wish I could give you something!" blurted Carlos, unable to hold the words in. "You have given me so much happiness. I wish that I could thank you with something besides words."

There was a silence all about the table. Ken looked surprised and doubtful. Mrs. Johnson gazed hard at Carlos, but there was a kind, gentle look in her eyes.

"A present," Mr. Johnson said at last. "But, Carlos, you've given us a present practically every day you've been here."

"I have?" Carlos looked puzzled. "What presents have I given you?"

"Why, you've given us hours of wonderful stories about your home and your family and your village. You've told us exciting Mexican legends and folk tales. Listening to your stories was almost like taking a guided tour through Mexico! You've shown us your country, with your words."

"That's right!" exclaimed Ken. "You showed me how to get water out of a barrel cactus in the desert, and how to make adobe for a shelter."

"And you gave us those recipes for tacos and beans," added Mrs. Johnson. "Everyone in the neighborhood has borrowed those recipes."

"But—" Carlos took a deep breath. "All of the things you say I've given you are Mexican things."

"And all the things you say we've given you are American things," laughed Mr. Johnson. "We've made a fair trade. We've each learned something we didn't know before."

Carlos jumped up. "I'll be right back," he said, and ran upstairs.

Quickly he returned to the dining room, the many-colored serape draped neatly across his arm. Yes, he understood now. His mother had been right.

"This is a gift from my family to your family," he said, placing the scrape on the table. "It's a Mexican serape. The designs on it are Indian signs."

"It's beautiful," sighed Mrs. Johnson, fingering it. "What do the signs mean, Carlos?"

Carlos smiled as he explained. "They are the signs of friendship." And as he looked into the faces of the Johnson family, he knew that he had given them the very best gift there was.

The Little Knitter

By Nelly M. Hudson

In the middle of the night, Joanna woke up. There had been an unusual sound somewhere in the house. It seemed to be coming from the kitchen, and it sounded like the creak of Grandma's rocking chair, followed by a very deep sigh. Then came a sound as if something dropped.

Joanna gathered up her courage, tiptoed down the stairs, and peeked into the kitchen. There was Grandma, fast asleep in her rocking chair. The fire had gone out, and on the floor was a pair of gleaming knitting needles with a half-finished, red woolen sock.

While Joanna was watching, Grandma woke up with a start, looked at the clock, and picked up her knitting with another of those deep sighs. Joanna could hear her talking to herself: "Oh dear, oh dear—how tired I am! Getting so slow these days . . . the socks never seem to get done. Need the money though . . . this cold weather, and the little ones growing so fast. My, but it's chilly in here! Might as well go to bed now that the fire's out. I'll get some more done tomorrow."

Grandma started to get up, and Joanna flew upstairs and back into bed. Then she started thinking. Grandma had been talking about the money she would get for those socks. They must be really poor if Grandma had to work so hard even late at night!

Joanna had known for a long time that they were not rich. They lived on the island of Marken in Holland, and Grandpa was a fisherman. Every day he went out in his boat on the Zuider Zee, a huge lake surrounding the island. Joanna's father had been a fisherman, too, but he and her mother had died many years ago. Ever since she could remember, Joanna and her small brother, Hans, had lived with their grandparents.

This winter had been bad for fishing. Frost had set in early, and the Zuider Zee had been frozen for almost two months now. Joanna loved skating, and so far she had enjoyed the winter very much indeed. Thinking about Grandma now, she began to realize that snow and frost were not all fun. No fishing for Grandpa, and poor Grandma had to work every night!

Suddenly an idea flashed through her mind. Suppose she did some knitting after Grandma had gone to bed? She slipped downstairs again, taking a blanket to wrap up in, and began to knit.

Like most girls on the island, Joanna had learned to knit at an early age. In every family there always seemed to be someone in need of something warm and new. Fathers and brothers who went fishing used thick homemade sweaters, scarves, and socks; and, in fact, everyone liked to dress warmly since the climate was so chilly. It was just part of being a Marken girl, doing your five or six rows each day, and Joanna was no exception. She was a quick worker, and two hours later the sock was finished. Then Joanna went back to bed, thinking happily about the big surprise Grandma would have when she came downstairs the next morning.

After breakfast Joanna heard Grandma say to Grandpa, "Peter, I must be getting my old speed back! Look how much knitting I did last night! This will really help us out till the frost is over if I can keep it up."

That evening Joanna set her alarm clock for midnight, wrapped it up in a sweater, and put it under her pillow so no one else would hear it. Again she knitted from midnight till three o'clock. She finished one sock, and even started another!

In the morning Grandma was humming to herself as she counted the finished socks. "Children, hot chocolate and *oliebollen* tonight!" she said. (*Oliebollen* are a treat in Holland, much like doughnuts.) Grandpa, too, was cheerful all day and after dinner told them stories of life at sea.

Joanna was so pleased with the results of her night work that she decided to keep it up till the frost would be over. After a week, however, she began to feel tired and she could hardly keep her eyes open in school. Her grades went down, and one morning she fell so fast asleep that the teacher had to shake her to wake her up. She was sent home with a note for Grandpa, who frowned terribly while he read it.

"Why can't you keep awake in school? And why have your grades gone down?" he asked. Joanna hung her head but didn't answer. "Very well," Grandpa said. "It's probably all this skating that makes you so tired. You'd better stay away from the ice for a while and study, young lady."

Joanna felt like crying but she thought, "If I tell them about the knitting now, they won't let me do any more."

So she continued working nights and trying to stay awake during the day. A few days later, however, she was so exhausted that she fell asleep over her knitting and never woke up till Grandma came into the kitchen the next morning. Grandma stared in surprise at the little girl in the rocking chair, then at the knitting. Suddenly she understood what Joanna had been doing. She called Joanna, Grandpa, Hans—all at the same time and all the while hugging her granddaughter.

"I'm proud of you, Joanna!" Grandpa said, beaming at her while little Hans danced around, making everybody laugh.

All of a sudden Joanna said, "Listen, Grandpa! It's thawing!" They flew to the window and saw she was right. Slow and steady drops of water came from the roof, where foot-long icicles were beginning to melt.

They looked at each other with laughing faces (and Grandma with a tear or two) until Grandpa shouted, "Hurrah for the best little knitter in the world!" He lifted Joanna on his shoulders and carried her around the room in triumph. As she looked down at her grandparents and her brother, Joanna knew she would never regret having worked so hard for the people she loved.

Don't Tell Maria

By Dorothy Babcock Phillips

Jessie peeked at the clock. Ten minutes to go. She groaned and started through her piece again, giving the piano keys an angry thump with each measure.

"Jessie, please!" Mother's voice came promptly from the kitchen.

Jessie swung around on the piano stool and burst into tears.

Mother appeared in the doorway. "Darling! What is it?"

"Oh, Mom, I hate practicing. I wish Grandma had never given us this ugly monster of a piano."

"Why, Jessie! You were so excited the day it arrived. You begged for lessons. Remember?"

"But I didn't know about scales and chords and ar—arpeggios. I didn't know I'd have to go over and over the same old piece. I keep making mistakes. Practicing is such hard work."

"Of course it is, Jessie, but someday . . ."

"I don't care about someday. Do I have to go on taking lessons? Please? I want to stop."

Mother looked serious. "That's a big decision, one we'll have to talk over. Right now, I want you to run upstairs and change your clothes. Maria is coming to dinner."

"She is?" Tears forgotten, Jessie hurried to her room. She could persuade Mom about the lessons. She knew she could. In the meantime, there would be the fun of seeing Maria.

Maria was their friendship student from the university. Jessie had met her once, at a reception for the exchange students, and she could hardly wait to see her again.

How beautiful Maria had looked when she was introduced from the front of the room—"Miss Maria Doria from the Philippines." She had responded to the clapping with such a friendly smile. And her dress! Jessie had never seen one like it before. A long green skirt and a white blouse with the most wonderful sleeves that stood up high and crisp against Maria's dark hair like the wings of a butterfly.

The doorbell rang. Jessie flew to answer it.

"Why, how do you do, Jessie. Do you remember me? We met at the reception, did we not? And you are wearing the same beautiful blue dress."

Jessie nodded, pleased that Maria had noticed, but she stared in disappointment at Maria's plain sweater and skirt. "I hoped you'd wear the same dress, too—the butterfly one."

Maria laughed. "The *mestisa* dress? That is what we call it, but that is for formal occasions. Your mother asked me to come as one of the family."

Jessie realized suddenly that their guest was still waiting on the doorstep. "Oh, please come in."

She led the way to the living room. In the doorway Maria stopped short and let her breath out in a long sigh. "You have a piano!"

Wondering, Jessie watched her cross the room, put out her hand, and touch the instrument. "Such a beautiful one," Maria said softly. "Do you play piano, Jessie?"

Jessie shook her head. No one could call the practicing she had to go through "playing."

"It belonged to my grandmother, but she moved to an apartment and gave it to us. Can you play?"

Maria nodded, "Oh, Jessie, do you suppose your mother would mind if . . . ?"

At that moment, Mother appeared in the doorway. "Maria! We're so happy that you could come to our home today."

"Maria would like to play our piano," Jessie told her mother.

Mother smiled. "Of course you must play our piano, Maria, whenever you wish. While you're at the university, please look on our home as yours. Why don't you sit down and play now? Jessie, you keep Maria company while I put the finishing touches on dinner. Dad will be home soon."

Maria slid onto the piano stool. She shook her head slowly, and Jessie was astonished to see tears in her eyes. "I thought it might be four years before I would touch a piano again. There is none in the dorm where I live." She began to play a lively march.

Jessie found that her feet would not keep still. Soon she was marching up and down behind Maria's back. Maria turned and caught her at it, and they laughed together.

Out of breath, Jessie dropped down on the couch. "How long did it take you to learn to play like that? Wasn't it awfully hard work?"

"Hard work? How long?" Maria looked puzzled. "I don't know. I don't remember. In our family there are twelve children. My father taught the first one. After that, we taught each other. I must have learned from my sister Luz, but I don't remember a time of not knowing. Our great problem is finding a time when the piano is not being played by someone else."

"Play some more," Jessie begged.

"Sometimes," Maria said, "we make up our own tunes. Like this." She began to play something that sounded like a lullaby. Curled in a corner of the couch, Jessie thought of rain falling softly outside as she lay warm and safe in bed.

A sound of clapping made them turn. Mother and Dad stood in the doorway smiling at them. "I hope we'll have more music after dinner," Mother said, "but now it's time to eat."

As the others left the room, Jessie lagged behind to stare at the piano. She ran her hand across the smooth, dark wood as she had seen Maria do.

"Jessie, we're waiting for you." It was Mother.

Jessie ran to her. "Oh, Mom," she begged in a low voice, "you won't tell Maria what I said about our piano, will you?"

Her mother smiled. "The ugly monster? No, I won't tell her. I promise."

"And, Mom, I've changed my mind about the lessons. The next time Maria comes, I'm going to play my piece for her."

Mother gave Jessie a quick hug. "And don't forget that Grandma's coming soon for a visit. She'll enjoy hearing it, too."

GULER TRAVELS ON TWO CONTINENTS

By Eve B. MacMaster

Guler woke up very excited that morning. It was the day she and her family would travel from their home in Istanbul to the town where Guler's grandmother lived.

Guler thought about the surprise she had for Grandmother. She had learned to read and write so well this year in school that she was taking some of her books and compositions to show Grandmother how well she was doing. These thoughts were so exciting that Guler jumped quickly out of bed and hurried into the kitchen to greet her mother.

"Good morning, my dear," said Mother with a hug and a kiss. "How is my little smiling one today?" Guler's name meant "smiling," and her parents often commented on how it suited her.

Mother was fixing their usual breakfast of bread, white cheese, black olives, and tea when Kemal and Papa came in.

"We need to hurry," said Papa. "My mother is expecting us for dinner. The bus from Uskudar will be crowded. We should be at the ferry station before nine, my dears." A smile crossed his moustached face. "We're traveling on two continents today, and we should be at your grandmother's before nightfall!"

Guler's family lived in Europe; Grandmother lived in Asia; but they all lived in Turkey, because Turkey is on two continents. The smaller, western part of the country is in Europe. It includes the city of Istanbul, and across the Bosporus is eastern Turkey and Asia. The Bosporus is a channel that links the Black Sea on the north to the Sea of Marmara on the south. Guler and her family planned to cross the Bosporus in a ferryboat. Although there was a new bridge across the channel, they still enjoyed the ferryboat ride.

Mother was fixing *boreks*—light pastries filled with cheese, meat, and spinach—to eat on the journey. She also had some sweet cakes for Grandmother. She wrapped these carefully in waxed paper and put them in a cardboard box.

Guler finished breakfast and put on the new dress and embroidered sweater her mother had made for her. She picked up her reading books and her composition notebook and carefully put them in her schoolbag. She stood by the front door waiting for the others.

It seemed like forever, but in a few minutes they were all ready and out of the apartment building. On the way to the taxicab stop they passed a row of shops. Guler's favorite was the candy store. She looked into the store's window as they passed.

Lokum, known to the rest of the world as "Turkish delight," was temptingly displayed in the center of the window. The lightly flavored squares of jellied candy were sweet, sticky delights. Guler especially liked the gritty *halvah* bars made from rice flour and ground sesame seeds. But today she knew there would be even more treats awaiting them at Grandmother's house.

They crossed the crowded city in a taxi and got out at the busy dockside on the Bosporus where the ferryboat was loading. Guler was fascinated by the sights near the ferry station. Big ships from all over the world were docked nearby, all with flags of different nations.

Vendors were calling out their wares in musical Turkish. "Fish, fresh fish!" "Oranges, apples, fruit!" "Sesame buns, fresh baked today!" Guler liked the sesame seed buns, hot from the bakery. She often bought one at school from the vendor who came by at recess.

Papa bought the tickets, and Kemal helped him carry their bags across the gangplank. Mother and Papa went to get some tea, telling Kemal to keep an eye on Guler. The ferry was crowded as usual, but the children found a place at the rail on the upper deck from which they could watch the crowd below and the city beyond them.

Too-oo-oot! The boat whistle warned that the ferry was about to leave. Guler couldn't feel any movement, but she saw the dock seem to grow smaller as it receded from them. The crowd on the dock paid no attention as the ferry slipped away. They were too busy buying, selling, and waiting for the next ferry.

Kemal leaned casually against the railing and looked down at his sister. "Well, Guler," he teased, "what do you expect to discover by staring so hard at the water? Sunken treasure?"

They laughed together.

"Oh, Kemal! I've brought my schoolbag. I want to show Grandmother all I've been learning at school. Do you think she will be pleased? Do you think there'll be time to show her my compositions?"

"Of course she will, Guler. Grandmother never went to school herself, and you know she's very proud of you."

While they were talking, the ferryboat landed at the Asiatic side of the Bosporus. Guler and Kemal went down to the lower deck to find their parents, and the whole family got off together.

They walked the short distance to the bus station and boarded the bus for Adapazari, a town that lay at the end of a two-hour bus ride. There Grandmother would be waiting.

The bus ride passed quickly. Guler watched out the window as towns of tile-roofed houses went by. In every town they passed there was at least one mosque. The minarets of the mosques were tall and slim, like giant pencils against the sky.

"Adapazari!" called the bus driver. Papa gathered their bags and found a phaeton as soon as they got off. The horse-drawn carriage and its sleepy driver seemed to be waiting just for them. Adapazari didn't have fast taxicabs like Istanbul, but Guler enjoyed the gentle clip-clop sound of the horse's hooves on the street. They turned a corner and Guler could see Grandmother's house, a small stucco building with a flat roof. And there in front was Grandmother herself! She wore the long, full skirts and long-sleeved blouse customary for women of her generation. Guler's mother, by contrast, was dressed in a trim suit.

"Ah, my dears!" said Grandmother with a wave. She reached up to lift Guler out of the carriage. "I kiss your eyes, little one," she said, and she did. Then she took the package of cakes from Mother and led the way into the house.

Guler could smell the roast mutton and rice and cakes and puddings. She would read to Grandmother after dinner and tell her some of the funny things that happened at school. She would draw a picture for her and write her name. She would . . .

"Well, look at Guler!" exclaimed Grandmother. "All this traveling has put my little one to sleep!" And she gathered up Guler in her arms and tucked her into a little cot.

The Broken Lantern

By A.S. Gleason

In the kitchen of their home in Norway, eleven-year-old Neils Holmen and his younger sister, Margita, played tag around the big table.

"Look out!" Neils shouted as Margita stumbled and fell, pulling the cloth and knocking the carefully polished lantern onto the floor.

"Oh, Neils!" Margita sobbed. "It's broken! What will I do?"

Neils stooped, carefully picking up the lantern pieces. It was a very special lantern made by their older brother, Gunnar. Around the base he had fastened five metal figures, one for each member of the family. These figures surrounding the lantern chimney were like a family holding together a warm home.

Soon Gunnar would be home again from the sea. How eagerly they had all waited for this time when the whole family would gather again. The warmth of the lantern always drew them closer together as they talked and laughed. The lantern was important to Gunnar's homecoming.

But now the chimney was broken. The five little figures were sadly bent. Margita continued to wail, for when Papa and Mama came home from the field they would know about the lantern.

"Everyone will know that I've spoiled Gunnar's homecoming!" Margita cried.

Neils examined the lantern again. There was a shop in Narvik that did repair work. But Neils shook his head, thinking, "I would need money to have the lantern mended. The only money I have is what I have been saving for new skates."

But when he thought of Margita and Gunnar's homecoming, he knew that the skates would have to wait.

Carefully carrying the broken lantern, Neils boarded the bus that traveled back and forth across the countryside. It left the village and headed for Narvik, the city on West Fjord.

The harbor in Narvik had always seemed exciting to Neils. And as he was about to enter the shop, the glinting water winked at him from the distance. Neils turned his back on it, even though he yearned to see the ships.

He greeted the shopkeeper. "Our lantern is broken. Can you mend it right away, please?"

"My helper is out," the man said, "and I have other jobs, too. It will take at least two hours."

Neils didn't protest. What would be wrong with spending those two hours at the harbor?

"I will be back," Neils said.

"Give me your name," the shopkeeper said, "so that I may put a tag on your lantern."

"The name is Holmen," said Neils, and he hurried out of the shop.

The harbor was as exciting as Neils had dreamed it would be. Ships of many sizes and from many countries were there. He watched for a long time.

"Soon Gunnar's boat will be in," Neils thought. The thought awoke him from his dreams and reminded him of his errand. He had forgotten the time. If he missed the last bus back to the village, he would not get the lantern home before his parents returned from the fields.

The clock in the shop told Neils that he was only a little late. He breathed a sigh, then noticed that there was a different man behind the counter.

"Where is the shopkeeper?" Neils asked.

"He is gone for the rest of the day," the man answered. "What can I do for you?"

"I have come for my lantern," Neils said. "It was to be repaired." He waited anxiously.

"Your name?" the man asked.

"Holmen," Neils answered. "H-O-L-M-E-N, Holmen. The shopkeeper wrote it on the tag."

The man looked up. "Was it a lantern with five figures? That has already been called for."

Neils felt a wave of heat rush to his head. "But that's impossible!" he cried out. "It was my family's lantern."

The man shrugged helplessly. "All I know is that a man already took the lantern."

"But don't you see!" Neils said. "The name was on the tag! Anyone could come in and say that his name was Holmen!"

"There is nothing I can do," the man said. "Sometimes these things happen."

Neils wanted to shout his anger, but the words wouldn't pass the knot in his throat. He walked away slowly, and his anger turned to guilt. If only he hadn't gone to the harbor! He had let Margita down, and Gunnar, too. Because of him the family had lost the special lantern.

Neils saw the bus leaving without him, but he didn't care. He would walk all the way home. He needed time to think.

But even the long walk didn't give him enough time. He reached home, and in the kitchen with the rest of the family sat his brother Gunnar. His face beamed at seeing Neils, and this made Neils feel even worse. He wanted to turn and run, but instead he threw himself into Gunnar's out-stretched arms.

"Gunnar, I have to tell you...," Neils started. Then his eye caught a gleam from the table. It was the lantern! Their very own lantern! With five straight figures and a new chimney.

"It was *you* who took the lantern from the shop!" Neils said to Gunnar.

"I'm sorry if you were worried, Neils," his brother said. "I had to wait for the bus to the village, so I spent the time browsing through the shops. I saw the lantern and knew it was ours. I brought it home, not thinking you had waited for it."

"It was only after Gunnar arrived home," Margita said, "that we knew what you had done, Neils." Her eyes flashed a warm look of thanks, while the lantern cast out a glow that drew the family around the table. They listened to stories about the sea, and they opened their gifts from Gunnar. For Mama, there was a colorful shawl; for Margita, a doll; and for Papa, a handsome pipe.

Then Neils opened his gift. He cried out at the sight of silver-bladed skates, and his heart burned brighter than the lantern.

Important
After All

By Eileen D. Za

One morning Jean-Luc Bedard woke up very early, just as the sun was beginning to peek through the shutters. Jean-Luc—who lived in the French village of Cap Breton with his three big brothers, his mother, and his father, who was a fisherman—hopped out of bed and hurried into the kitchen, where his mother was putting hot rolls on the table for breakfast.

"*Maman*," asked Jean-Luc as he rubbed his eyes, "is today the day?"

"Yes, my dear," answered his mother as Jean-Luc took his place at the table next to *Papa.* "Today is July 14th, the greatest day in French history, and an important national holiday."

"And the day I get to stay up late. Right, *Papa?*"

Monsieur Bedard laughed. "Right. Now you are old enough to enjoy all the fun and games. So tonight you may stay up late and see the *Toro del Fuego,* the mighty Bull of Fire."

Jean-Luc smiled with delight. He had seen the bicycle race, even the *pelota* championship, and the street dance that began at dusk when the village band paraded through the streets, gathering all the people behind it like children behind the Pied Piper. All these he had seen and enjoyed. But never had he seen the glorious Bull of Fire.

"Once," explained Monsieur Bedard, "there were real bullfights here in Cap Breton. But long ago the people gave them up in favor of a beautiful bull they made themselves—a bull covered with the bright glow from thousands of fireworks. Unfortunately, the bull is only allowed out late at night when it is very dark and all the little children are fast asleep. But now that you're seven, Jean-Luc, you may stand in the square with your brothers and watch the *Toro del Fuego.*"

How slowly the day passed! Tagging along behind his brothers, Jean-Luc ran first to the corner to watch the bicycle race. Round and round the village young men rode, crouched low over their handlebars, trying so hard to win the big silver cup that would sit in the parlor for the rest of the year.

"I wish *Papa* would enter the race," Jean-Luc said to his brothers. "How proud I would be. But he never does anything exciting."

The *pelota* game was fast and furious as the two finalists leaped and ran, catching the hard rubber ball in long wicker baskets strapped to their right arms and throwing it back against the concrete wall with all their might.

"I wish *Papa* were better at *pelota*," sighed Jean-Luc as he watched a lovely lady put a garland of flowers around the winner's neck while everyone cheered. "Wouldn't it be great if he won the championship and everyone clapped and cheered for him!"

After dinner *Maman* and Jean-Luc and the three big brothers hurried out to watch the band go by. Playing a happy tune, they stepped out smartly—one, two, one, two—while the big bass drum beat out the rhythm.

"I wish *Papa* played in the band," said Jean-Luc wistfully. "A person must be important when he leads the parade!"

"You should be very proud of your father," *Maman* told her young son. "He's a fine man."

"I know. But he never does anything exciting."

As the bigger boys ran on ahead, Jean-Luc and his mother strolled along to the square, where a large crowd had already gathered.

"Let's stand near the edge, Jean-Luc," suggested *Maman*. "We'll be able to see better from there."

The two of them stood hand in hand, awaiting the arrival of the *Toro del Fuego*. Jean-Luc was not quite sure what to expect. When the crowd yelled "Here it comes!" he quivered with excitement.

"Are you nervous?" asked his mother.

"Of course not," answered Jean-Luc. "But I wish *Papa* were here. Where is he? He'll miss the fun."

His mother had no time to answer, for there, right in the middle of the square, was the bull, sparkling and glowing with hundreds of brilliant fireworks that were attached to its broad back. A wooden frame held up the huge head, which had whirling wheels for eyes and two large rockets waiting to take off, just where its horns should be.

"Oh, *Maman*," sighed Jean-Luc, "I've never seen anything so beautiful. But where is *Papa?* Why isn't he with us?"

"He'll come soon," said Madame Bedard. "He wouldn't miss the *Toro del Fuego* for anything."

Suddenly the bull put down its head and pretended to charge the crowd, which squealed and laughed and backed away, pretending to be very frightened. Some of the bigger boys—Jean-Luc's brothers were among them—took off their jackets and flapped them in front of the bull like imaginary capes.

"*Toro, toro,*" the boys called, just like the real bullfighters. And the bright bull ambled off after them as fast as its four legs could carry it, with fireworks of every shape and size and color crackling and popping and sparkling along its sides. The bull was truly a breath-taking sight.

"Oh, what fun!" laughed Jean-Luc, clapping his hands and stamping his feet with the rest of the crowd. "I DO wish *Papa* were here."

Finally the last rocket sailed off into the dark night and burst into glittering umbrella of bright green stars.

"Aah," sighed the crowd, for they knew it was all over.

"Aah," sighed Jean-Luc, too. "It's over, and *Papa* missed it all."

"Oh, no, he didn't," smiled his mother. "See, here he comes now."

Jean-Luc could see nothing but the big bull shape coming toward them. Slowly the front half detached itself from the rear. Two arms came out from underneath the canvas covering and lifted off the heavy head.

And there underneath the bulky costume was *Papa,* laughing at the surprised look on Jean-Luc's face! Monsieur Bedard was the front legs and head of the *Toro del Fuego!*

"Oh, *Papa,*" cried Jean-Luc, "I thought you were going to miss all the fun. But you were really the most exciting part of the whole day. You must be important after all!"

Sea Legs

By Phyllis Feuerstein

From his perch on the sampan, Chien Hung could see the shore. It was as dotted with people as the harbor was jammed with boats. Hung felt himself become tense as he imagined trying again to walk on land.

He sighed and brought his attention back to the sampan village. It was noisy with farewells. Boys like himself, born on the waters, were going ashore for the first time. If they were worried about walking on solid ground, they hid it well.

They acted eager. All but Hung, who had tried once before. And he should have been the most eager, because his father had been the first one of them to go ashore and start the school.

Chien Hung was proud that his father could tread firmly where the marketplace was thick with people, rickshas, cars, and taxis. But Hung was ashamed of himself. He still could not accustom himself to the idea of walking without the feel of the rise and fall of the sea water beneath his feet.

Hung knew his father wished he would lose his fear. Hung wished it, too, but wishing didn't erase the memory of his only time ashore.

Plague had threatened Hong Kong. People from all parts rushed to be vaccinated. Hung was little then. When his father set him down, he walked on sea legs from side to side, instead of forward, and fell. Hurrying feet almost trampled him. His father scooped him up in time. But now, when Hung was asked to go ashore, he stiffened with fear.

Hung's father hurried forward. Beaming with excitement, he put an arm around the boy's shoulders. "By noon," he said, "the boys will be there. For a while they'll walk wobbly. Then they'll get their land legs and walk straight ahead to school."

His father's excitement was catching. Hung's eyes brightened.

"The school is above a stall where a woman sells roast duck," Mr. Wong said cheerfully. "And perhaps tomorrow you'll be there with all the other boys.

"But for now," his father continued when Hung stiffened, "you can come as far as the pier and wait in the scow to take me home."

"Will May Chi keep me company?" Hung asked.

His father looked thoughtful. "Yes," he said after a pause. "But keep your eyes on her—especially when she's quiet. That's the time she's thinking of doing something she shouldn't."

Hung helped unfasten the scow that the sampan towed. Then May Chi, his little sister, was lowered into the scow. "Time to go," Chi called eagerly. "Come on, Hung!"

Hung held on to Chi while his father poled the scow. Soon Chi grew drowsy, leaving Hung free to gaze across the junks and sampans and barges at the clearly outlined mainland. "Does it feel strange to walk without the movement of water beneath your feet?" he asked fearfully.

His father nodded. "Very strange at first. But I go ashore often and get my land legs quickly. You will, too, sometime soon."

Chien Hung shook his head and inched as far back in the scow as he could when they neared the plank reaching up to the land. Even seeing those wooden boards made him stiffen with fright.

Hung's father secured the scow and climbed the planks; they moved under his weight. Hung watched him and held his breath. His father swayed on sea legs a moment or two, turned to wave good-bye, and walked forward.

Hung felt frightened just watching. Soon his father was out of sight. He was about to look at Chi when voices above the pier commanded attention. "Take you ashore! One dollar!" Small boys called down to visitors touring the harbor. They ran freely, making Hung feel more ashamed.

He stood on tiptoe. Now the ricksha men cried, "Take you somewhere!" Then a peasant woman called, "Time! Time! Sell you a watch!" Hung felt better. These were people born on land. For a minute he had thought he was the only one besides Chi who wasn't ashore.

Chi! Hung remembered his little sister and spun around. The scow was empty. Chi had scrambled from the moored scow to a sampan and then onto another plank. She teetered at its top. Hung was so scared he couldn't speak. He stood like a statue while Chi waved her red scarf at him and tottered onto the pier and into the crowd.

"Chi!" he managed to call. Chi did not return. Hung knew he must go after her. Nobody from the sampan village knew Chi was ashore. The boys and his father were already at school. Chi was wobbling on land among all those moving people.

Hung thought of his gentle little sister as he stared up at the plank. Anything might happen to

Chi. She might get lost and never find her way back. She might fall and be trampled. He took a deep breath and clambered up the plank. The ricksha men and small boys stared at him as he swayed on the pier. "Did you see a small girl holding a red scarf?" he asked them.

They hadn't, but the peasant woman pointed down a narrow street. Hung could see hundreds of people milling about where the sidewalks were lined with stalls. Then he thought he saw the flutter of a red scarf. Chi! He walked like a crab from side to side into the thick crowd.

At the busy corner at the end of the street, he thought he saw the red scarf fly into the traffic. He saw Chi follow the scarf. Hung's heart pounded. He could tell Chi didn't realize she was in danger. She chased the scarf.

Hung ran between two rickshas and then between two taxis. He fell and picked himself up. "Chi, stand still! I'm coming."

A policeman who stood on a high platform facing the opposite direction heard Hung's shouting. The policeman blew his whistle, and the threatening traffic stopped.

Hung reached his little sister. Tears fell from her eyes like raindrops. "I've lost my red scarf." She cried as if heart would break.

"We'll find Father," Hung said, "and get you another one."

Suddenly Chien Hung realized what he had done. He had walked on land! He'd even run between taxis and rickshas when Chi had chased her red scarf. He wasn't scared anymore. And he had walked a longer distance than his friends who had left earlier in the day.

Soon Hung and Chi were at the stall where the woman sold roast duck. Hung looked up at the rooftop where his friends were studying. "Father, I'm here," he wanted to shout. Instead he gripped Chi's hand tightly and searched for a stall that might have a red scarf. Later he would explain to his father how Chi had lost her red scarf and how he had found his land legs.

ONE MORE O'GRADY

By Gail Tepperman Barclay

When the square blue envelope that had come all the way from America arrived at the post office, Jim Duffy, the mail carrier, delivered it to the O'Grady cottage himself.

"Sure, it's an important-looking letter, you mark my words," said Jim Duffy, and he held out the envelope to Mother O'Grady. But she was up to her elbows in the bread dough she was kneading.

"Mary, you take the letter and tell Mr. Duffy thank you for bringing it," said Mother O'Grady.

And so Mary was the one who got to open the envelope and unfold the letter that was inside. "It smells good," said Mary, holding the paper to her nose and sniffing the violet perfume that Aunt Annie always sprayed on her letters.

"Flowers are for smelling and letters are for reading," said Mother. "What does it say?"

Mary read the letter. "She says that she has room for one more O'Grady, now that she has bought a bigger house. She wants to know which one of us you're going to send."

"Does she, now?" Mother wiped the sticky white dough from her hands and took the letter. "One more O'Grady," mused Mother when she'd read the letter through twice. "Who shall it be?"

That night after supper, all the O'Grady children sat at the table while Father stood off to one side and listened to Mother read Aunt Annie's letter.

"Who shall it be?" asked Mother when she'd done reading.

"Umm, hmm." Father gazed at the six children. "Who would most like to go to America and live with Aunt Annie?"

Tim was the oldest, and he spoke first. "Well, I'd like to go. But since I'm the oldest boy, it just wouldn't be right for me to leave. But perhaps Mike or Teddy could go."

"Teddy's older than me," said Mike. "It wouldn't be fair for me to go and Teddy to stay."

"I don't think I'd better go either," said Teddy slowly. "If I go to America, who's going to keep Mike company?"

"It ought to be one of the girls," said Tim thoughtfully. "How about you, Mary?"

Mary sighed. "I would love to go and live in America," she said, "but I know that Mother needs me, and so I'd better stay here. But Susan or Kathleen could go."

"Is America like Ireland?" asked Kathleen, who was the youngest of the O'Gradys.

"America isn't like any place in the world except America," said Father. "It's a wonderful place. You could have almost anything you want. In America nearly every family has two cars. You would probably have your own to drive, Tim."

"That would be grand," Tim said, imagining his own car.

"And in the cities there are hundreds of different shops," added Mary.

"I'll tell you what," said Mother. "There's only one fair way to decide which of you six children goes to live with Aunt Annie, and this is how we'll do it. Each of you write your own name on a slip of paper and put it in Father's hat. Then I'll close my eyes, and the name I pick out will be the one who goes."

Mary ran to get the slips of paper, Tim found six pencils, and little Kathleen fetched Father's hat from its peg in the corner. Each of the six O'Gradys took a slip of paper and then folded the paper over and over again. Then Teddy passed around the hat, and each O'Grady put his or her folded slip of paper inside.

At last everything was ready for Mother to pick the winning name. She closed her eyes, reached into the hat, and picked out one slip of paper. The children held their breath as Mother opened her eyes, unfolded the paper, and prepared to read the name of the lucky child.

"Why, look at this!" exclaimed Mother. "There's nothing written on this paper." She showed them. "Nothing at all. Well, I'll just pick out another one."

But when she unfolded it, the second slip of paper was as blank as the first.

"Pick another," advised Father.

But the third piece of paper was blank, too!

"Goodness!" Mother exclaimed, unfolding the other three slips of paper. "They're all blank!"

The six O'Gradys looked at one another and didn't say a word.

"But in America you children would have so much. Your aunt would buy you the best clothes. She would take you to the movies. When you're older, you could choose the university you want to attend." Father walked back and forth in front of them. "Why, I can think of six good reasons for you to go!" he said, stopping in front of Susan.

"And I can think of seven good reasons for me to stay right here," she replied. "They're Tim and Mike and Teddy and Mary and Kathleen and Mother and—" Susan looked him straight in the eye, "and you! That's seven things I won't have if I go, and those are the seven best things in the world for me."

"Me, too!" cried out Tim.

"Me, too!" added Mary.

"Me, too!" shouted Teddy and Mike.

"Me, too!" piped Kathleen.

Father said, "Harrumph!"

Mother blinked and wiped her eyes. "And so none of you wrote down your names," she said. "Well, I suppose I'll have to write to Aunt Annie and tell her that we just don't have any O'Gradys to spare."

And that's exactly what she did.